The *Bing* television series is created by Acamar Films and Brown Bag Films and adapted from the original books by Ted Dewan.

Bing's Yellow Wellies is based on the original story *Wellies* written by An Vrombaut, Lucy Murphy and Mikael Shields. It was adapted from the original story by Rebecca Gerlings.

Bing's Ice Lolly is based on the original story *Ice Lolly* written by Tracey Hammett, Lucy Murphy, Mikael Shields, Ted Dewan and An Vrombaut. It was adapted from the original story by Rebecca Gerlings.

Bing's Acorn Hunt is based on the original story *Acorns* written by An Vrombaut, Lucy Murphy, Mikael Shields and Ted Dewan. It was adapted from the original story by Rebecca Gerlings.

Dragon Breath is based on the original story written by Ted Dewan, Lucy Murphy, Mikael Shields and An Vrombaut. It was adapted from the original story by Rebecca Gerlings.

First published in Great Britain by HarperCollins *Children's Books* in 2021
HarperCollins *Children's Books* is a division of HarperCollins*Publishers* Ltd
1 London Bridge Street, London SE1 9GF

www.harpercollins.co.uk

HarperCollins*Publishers*
1st Floor, Watermarque Building, Ringsend Road, Dublin 4, Ireland

1 3 5 7 9 10 8 6 4 2

ISBN: 978-0-00-846379-3

Printed and bound in Italy by Rotolito

MIX
Paper from
responsible sources
FSC™ C007454

FSC
www.fsc.org

This book is produced from independently certified FSC™ paper
to ensure responsible forest management.

For more information visit: www.harpercollins.co.uk/green

Spring Story
Bing's Yellow Wellies

Round the corner, not far away,
Flop has **a job** for Bing today!

It's a **wet spring** day, and Flop is tidying the kitchen.

"Can I help?" Bing asks.

"Sure!" replies Flop. "We need to take the rubbish out."

"OK, Flop. I'm a **good helper!**" says Bing.

Flop opens the front door. "Oh," he says. "It's been raining. Let's put your wellies on, Bing."

"Hello, wellies!" says Bing. "I've got a job for you – you have to come outside and keep my feet dry!"

"That's right. Your feet will be nice and snug in there," agrees Flop.

Bing slips on his
yellow wellies.
Now he's ready!

He drops the rubbish
bag into the big
bin outside.

FLUMP!

"Urgh!" says Bing.
"Smelly and 'sgusting!"

"Yup," chuckles Flop.
"Rubbish can get a bit
disgusting! Let's
close the lid now."

Flop explains that his box of rubbish is for recycling.

"What's reclycling?" asks Bing.

"*Recycling*," chuckles Flop. "Well, some things don't need to be thrown away. They can be made into new things: like cups, or buckets – or even loo brushes!"

Bing laughs. "Oh, clever bottle!"

It's time to go back indoors,
but Bing notices the rainy puddles!

"My wellies want to go this way," says Bing,
splish-splashing round the corner into the garden.

"What's that?" Bing gasps. There are some shiny trails on the ground.

"Let's go and find out," suggests Flop.

Bing and Flop follow the trails all the way to . . .

17

. . . some snails!

"Flop, why are
there so many
snails?" asks Bing.

"Snails like it when it's wet,"
Flop replies. "And so do the flowers."

"Like my wellies!" says Bing. "They love getting wet!"

19

Bing *splishes*
and *splashes*
round the garden
until he spots a
bucket of water.

"Let's do a
big splash,
wellies!"
he shouts.

JUMP!

"OH NO!"
says Bing . . .

. . . "My foot's all wet!"

"Oh, Bing!" says Flop.
"Let's have a look."

Flop takes Bing's welly off.

"Oh dear," he says, pointing
to a hole. "See? That's
where the water got in."

"Um . . . can
you fix it, Flop?"
Bing asks.

"I don't think I can,"
says Flop. "It may
be time for a new
pair of wellies."

"But I love my wellies!
Don't throw them away!"
says Bing, remembering
the smelly bin. "My wellies
won't like that!"

"OK," says Flop. "We won't put them in the bin.
Maybe we can find them a new job."

"What sort of new job?" asks Bing, hugging his welly.

"Let's go and have a look, shall we?" answers Flop.
"But let's take that drippy sock off first."

Flop tugs and tugs until the soggy sock comes off.

"That's better!"
says Flop.

Bing has one welly on and one bare
foot. He jumps on the wet grass.
"It feels lovely, Flop!" he says.
Splish! Splish! Splish!

Flop follows Bing on the
stepping stones. He doesn't
want to get his feet wet.

Hup! Hup! Hup!

29

Back by the flowerpots, Bing has an idea.
"Snail! I've got you **a new house!**" he says.
He waves his welly.

"I think snail likes his shell house," says Flop.

"Oh . . ."
says Bing,
having
another
idea.

Flop watches
as he picks up
a flowerpot . . .

31

. . . and puts
it inside his
broken welly!

"Look!" says Bing.
"It fits! I found
a new job
for welly!"

"You've recycled your welly into a welly pot," admires Flop. "Good for you, Bing Bunny!"

Bing laughs. "And good for you too, welly!"

Recycling . . . it's a Bing thing!

Summer Story
Bing's Ice Lolly

Round the corner, not far away,
Bing and Flop are **hot** today!

It's so warm today! Flop and Bing are filling the paddling pool to help them cool down.

"I want it to be full **right up to the top!**" says Bing.
"Can you make it fill up quick, Flop?"

"I can't, Bing," replies Flop.
"It's going to take a while."

Bing hears Gilly's ice cream van arrive!

"Gilly!" calls Bing.

Bing and Flop rush out to see her.
"Hello, Gilly!"

"Hello, Bing!
Hello, Flop!"
says Gilly.
"What will you
pick today?"

Bing studies the
pictures of lollies
and ice creams
on Gilly's van.

"Um . . . I'd like a
**juicy orange
fruit one**, please!"
decides Bing.

"What about
you, Flop?"

"Two juicy orange,
please," says Flop.

Bing and Flop find a shady spot in the garden to enjoy their lollies while the pool fills up.

SPLASH!

"What was that?" asks Bing.

Bing and Flop take a look. There's something in the paddling pool . . . **it's Froggy!**

"She must be feeling hot like us," says Flop, looking in.

"Yes!" agrees Bing. "And she wants to splash in the water."

45

"She might need us to help her," explains Flop.

Bing picks up his blue bucket. "I can help her!" he says.

"That's a good idea,"
replies Flop.
"Let's just put these
lollies down."

Flop places the lollies
on a plate in the shade.

"Let's be gentle
so Froggy doesn't
get hurt," says Flop.

Bing follows Froggy round
the pool. "She swam away!"
he exclaims.

"Hmm, maybe Froggy's scared,
Bing?" says Flop. "If you hold
your bucket statue-still
then she might just
come to you."

Bing tries again.
This time he stays statue-still . . .

It works! Froggy swims into Bing's blue bucket.

"Well done, Bing!" says Flop.

Bing and Flop take the bucket into the shade and let Froggy jump into her cool pipe.

"I did it!" Bing says proudly. "I helped Froggy!"

"Good for you, Bing Bunny," replies Flop.

52

But when Bing and Flop
go back to their ice lollies . . .

"My lolly!"
says Bing.
"What happened,
Flop? It's all
gone away!"

"Oh. Well, while we were helping Froggy,
the sun melted it," replies Flop.

Bing feels disappointed. "Oh, I wanted my ice lolly!" he says.

"I know, I wanted mine too," replies Flop. "Gilly's gone now,
but let's see what we can find inside . . ."

Flop suggests some juicy raspberries.

"They're not icy, Flop," says Bing.

"Well, we do have ice," says Flop, fetching some from the freezer.

Bing has an idea. "Can we mix them together?" he asks.

"Great idea!" says Flop. "Let's put everything in Brenda the blender!"

Bing tips in the raspberries
and Flop adds the ice. Then they
press Brenda's button . . .

"Let's go, go, go, go, goooo!"

"Icy raspberries – yum, yum, yum!" sings Bing, while Brenda mixes everything together.

"It *does* look icy," agrees Flop, showing him the mixture. "And fruity."

"Oh, raspberry mushy! Yum, yum, yum!" exclaims Bing, hopping from foot to foot in excitement.

"That's a good name!" chuckles Flop. "One raspberry mushy for you, and one for me."

"Let's drink them in the **paddling pool,** Flop!" suggests Bing.

"Good idea, Bing!" says Flop, as they head outside into the summer sunshine.

63

Ice lollies . . . they're a Bing thing!

Autumn Story
Bing's Acorns Hunt

Round the corner, not far away,
Bing is playing **I-spy** with Sula today.

Bing glances around the park. "I spy with my little eye, something coloured . . . red!" he says.

Sula looks up and spots something red drifting down to the ground.

"Um . . . is it a leaf?" she asks as it lands beside her.

"Yes!" Bing replies.

"Well spied, Sula!" says Flop.

Bing wonders why
all the trees are
different colours.

"It's autumn. The trees are getting ready for winter," explains Flop. "Their leaves change colour and fall down from the trees."

71

"Come on, Bing!" shouts Sula.
"Let's see if we can find any more!"

"Yes! I'm going to find lots!" calls Bing.

Sula is first to spot the next acorn.

"That's a **funny hat** you're wearing, Mr Acorn," she giggles, holding it in the air.

Bing and Flop search the ground together.

"We've found some more too!" calls Bing.

Bing lines
up all the
acorns
they've
found on
the ground.

"One, two,
three, four,
five, six!
Six acorns!"
he counts.

Bing and
Sula run off
to search for
more acorns.
Behind Flop,
something rustles
in the tree.

It's a squirrel! And he's *very* interested in Bing and Sula's acorns.

"Hmm," says Flop.

Bing and Sula return to add more acorns, but they're puzzled to find their collection isn't growing.

"One, two, three, four, five, six," they count together.

"Where have
they gone, Flop?"
asks Bing.

"Well, how about we try
to find out?" replies Flop.
"Let's hide behind that
bush over there."

Safely hidden, Bing and Sula listen excitedly
while Flop gives them some advice.

"OK," he whispers.
"We all need to stay mousey quiet."

Bing and Sula
slowly peep
over the top
of the bush.

"Now," says Flop,
pointing over to the
tree. "What can
you spy?"

"I can't spy anything,
Flop!" exclaims Bing.

"Not yet. Just wait
a minute," reassures
Flop. "Let's see
what happens."

Bing gasps! "I spy with my little eye . . ."

"A squirrel!" finishes Sula.

The squirrel is taking one
of Bing and Sula's acorns!

Sula thinks the squirrel is very cheeky.

"He's eating another one!" she says.

"I don't think he's eating that one, Sula," replies
Flop. "Come on, let's spy some more . . ."

Everyone watches quietly as
the squirrel hides the acorn
under some autumn leaves.

Once he's finished,
he scampers away to
collect some more.

"Why does the squirrel need so many acorns, Flop?" asks Bing.

"Maybe he's saving them for later," replies Flop.

Acorns . . . they're a Bing thing!

Bing

Winter Story
Dragon Breath

Round the corner,
not far away,
Bing and Pando
are playing in the
cold today!

Pando has come to play in Bing's garden on a cold winter's day.

"Look!" Bing says, puffing his breath into the chilly air. "I'm a dragon! RAAAR!"

"I'm a train!" cries Pando, joining in. "CHOO-CHOO!"

Bing and Pando are so excited about their new trick they rush indoors to show Flop.

"Flop! I've got **dragon breath!**" says Bing. "See?"

He puffs out . . .

. . . but the dragon breath is gone!

"Why isn't it working, Flop?" Bing asks.

"Because it's all warm inside," explains Flop.
"Try outside in the cold. Look at Pando."

Bing goes back into the garden with Flop. He tries again.

"There it is!" he cheers.
"I'm a dragon – RAAAR!"

"Brrr!" says Flop. "It's cold
enough out here for all of us
to have cloudy breath!"

Flop goes back inside to get his woolly hat and scarf.

While Flop's gone, Bing and Pando notice something hanging from the garden tap.

"What is it, Bing?" asks Pando.

Bing reaches out to touch it.
"Ooh! It's all icy cold!" he says.

Pando has
a go too.
"Oof! It's freezing!"

Bing snaps it off to show Flop.

"You found a beautiful icicle," says Flop.
He passes it back to Bing.

Bing holds it up. It sparkles in the light.

"Yes, beautiful," he admires. "But my hands are **all icy cold!**"

"How about some hot chocolate?" suggests Flop. "To warm us all up."

"Yay! Hot chocolate!" says Bing.

Bing brings the icicle inside.
He wants to keep it.

"Hmm . . . it won't stay icy for long
in the warm," says Flop. He places
it on a plate and opens the freezer.
"So how about we put it here?"

"Night-night, icicle!"
says Pando, waving.

While Flop's back is turned, Bing reaches for his hot chocolate.

"Wait a minute!" exclaims Flop. "It's still too **burny hot** to drink! It needs to cool down a little."

"But my hands are still cold," replies Bing.

Flop rubs Bing's hands to warm them up.
"We made a hand sandwich!"
giggles Bing.

"A toasty one!"
agrees Flop.

Bing can't wait for his hot chocolate any longer.

While Flop is rubbing Pando's hands,
he decides to test if it's ready to drink . . .

. . . with
his fingers!

"OWWW!"
cries Bing.
"It's all burny,
Flop!"

113

"Ooh! That's a bit too hot for your fingers. Come on, let's cool them down," says Flop.

He leads Bing towards the sink. "We need something cool to take that heat away," he explains.

"What about
that icicle?"
suggests Pando.

"Good idea, Pando,"
replies Flop.
"As long as we
are careful!"

Flop fetches the icicle
from the freezer.
"Here, Bing," he says,
handing it to him. "Hold
this. How does that feel?"

"Ooh . . . cold!"
smiles Bing.

"Good for you, Bing
Bunny," says Flop.
"That icicle has cooled
down the heat
in your hands."

That gives Bing an idea.

"Ooh!" he gasps.
"Can we put
some ice in
our hot chocolate?"

"Sure!" agrees Flop.

He fetches some clean ice from the freezer. Everyone takes a cube and drops it into their hot chocolate.

PLIP! PLOP! PLIP!

"Ooh! Icy hot chocolate!" laughs Pando.

"Look, Flop!" Bing gasps. "The ice is getting little! It's melting in the hot chocolate! Can we drink it now?"

Flop tests his first. "Mmm! Yes, it's just right," he says.

Bing, Flop and Pando take big gulps of their yummy-delicious hot chocolate.

SLURRRP!

"Mmm . . . yum!
My tummy's all warm," giggles Bing. "Can we go back outside, Flop?"

"Sure," Flop replies. "Now we've got some warm in our tummies it won't feel so cold."

"Come on, Pando!" shouts Bing. "Let's go!"

Being patient . . . it's a Bing thing!

SPRING

SUMMER

AUTUMN

WINTER